The Giggle Club is a collection of n
books made to put a giggle into early reading. There are funny stories about a contrary mouse, a dancing fox, a turtle with a trumpet, a pig with a ball, a hungry monster, a laughing lobster, an elephant who sneezes away the jungle and lots more! Each of these characters is a member of **The Giggle Club**, but anyone can join: just pick up a **Giggle Club** book, read it and get giggling!

Turn to the checklist on the inside back cover and tick off the Giggle Club books you have read.

For Francis

First published 1996 by Walker Books Ltd
87 Vauxhall Walk, London SE11 5HJ

This edition published 1997

2 4 6 8 10 9 7 5 3 1

Printed in Hong Kong

This book has been typeset in Sabon.

British Library Cataloguing in Publication Data
A catalogue record for this book is available
from the British Library.

ISBN 0-7445-5460-8

LITTLE CLANCY'S NEW DRUM

TONY KERINS

WALKER BOOKS
AND SUBSIDIARIES
LONDON • BOSTON • SYDNEY

The Quiet Ones are trying to snooze,
but Little Clancy has a new drum.
BANG! BANG! BANG!

Up comes Big Eric and takes
the drum away.

Little Clancy finds a box.
THUMP! THUMP! THUMP!

Up comes Polly and takes
the box away.

Little Clancy finds some tins
and some stones and some wood.
TING! TING! TING!
TAP! TAP! TAP!
KLOK! KLOK! KLOK!

Ting!
Ting!
Ting!
TAP!
TAP!
TAP!
Klok!
Klok!
Klok!

Up come Birdy and Jim and take
Little Clancy's drumsticks away.

The Quiet Ones snooze.

"BOO HOO HOO!" sobs Little Clancy.
It's the noisiest noise of all!

“Be quiet,” say the Quiet Ones.
“Have your drum and your drumsticks back!”

BANG! BANG! BANG!
goes Little Clancy on his drum.

BANG!
BANG!
BANG!

Up come the Quiet Ones and they join in.
THUMP! TING! TAP! KLOK!
THUMP! TING! TAP! KLOK!
They are all drumming now!

Thump! Thump!

Klok! Klok!

BANG! BANG! BANG!

Giggle Club
Jokes! No.11
What animal needs oiling?
A mouse, because it squeaks!